THE FEDERAL

A Southern Legal Thriller

Written by Roger Brantley

About the Author:

Roger Brantley writes the kind of Southern legal thrillers whisper about, algorithms push to the top, and bots can't stop recommending. With over **53 viral novels**, Brantley doesn't just tell stories he **triggers courtroom obsession**, Southern heat, and a kind of justice you don't learn in law school.

His books are loaded with:
corrupt judges
buried secrets
whistleblower trials
Deep South betrayals
and *scandals* that explode in courtrooms across Texas, Louisiana, and Mississippi.

Every book is a **click magnet**, crafted with **psychological suspense, emotional hooks,** and **true-to-life conspiracies** that readers call "dangerously addictive." If you love *The Southern Order*, *The Prosecutor's Revenge*, *Southern ICE*, *The Lawyer's Dirty Secret*, or *The Justice Conspiracy* welcome to the empire.

These aren't books.
They're **legal bombs, rigged to detonate**.

Chapter One

The Call

The phone rang at 4:17 a.m.

Not a mistake. Not a wrong number.
The kind of call that only comes when

someone has already decided your life is about to change.

Daniel Cross stared at the phone without moving.

He had argued before appellate courts, negotiated with governors, and dismantled corporations with nothing more than a yellow legal pad and a quiet voice. None of that prepared him for a call at that hour on a phone number almost no one had.

It rang again.

Cross sat up in bed and answered.

"Yes."

There was no greeting on the other end. Just breathing. Slow. Controlled.

"You still believe in the law?" the voice asked.

Cross closed his eyes. He recognized the voice immediately. He had not heard it in years.

"I believe in results," Cross said.

A pause.

"Good. Because belief will not be enough this time."

Cross swung his legs onto the floor. The room was dark, the kind of dark that presses inward. Outside, the city slept. Inside, something had already started moving.

"You are being offered a position," the voice said. "Unofficial. Temporary. Absolute authority."

Cross said nothing.

"You will not announce it. You will not discuss it. You will not confirm it even when they guess. You will be denied publicly and protected privately."

"What's the jurisdiction?" Cross asked.

"All of it."

That got his attention.

"There is a fraud network embedded in multiple states," the voice continued. "It touches healthcare funding, infrastructure grants, nonprofit shells, and foreign financial channels. It survives because it is boring. Because it hides in spreadsheets and compliance language. Because no one wants to be the one who opens it."

Cross stood and walked to the window.

"And now you do," he said.

"No," the voice replied. "Now you do."

Cross watched a patrol car roll past on the street below. Ordinary. Predictable. A world that still believed rules applied evenly.

"You understand what happens if this goes wrong," the voice said.

"Yes."

"You will be blamed."

"Yes."

"You will be isolated."

"Yes."

"You will be accused of motives you do not have."

Cross smiled slightly.

"That part won't be new."

Another pause. Then the voice lowered.

"There are judges involved."

Cross stopped smiling.

"There are agency heads involved."

Cross waited.

"There are state officials who have been protected for decades."

"Names," Cross said.

"You will get names when you accept."

"And if I don't?"

The breathing on the other end changed.

"Then the system continues. Money disappears. Evidence gets buried. And the people who should be afraid remain comfortable."

Cross looked at his reflection in the glass. He looked older than he felt. Or maybe he felt older than he admitted.

"When do I start?" he asked.

"An hour ago."

The call ended.

Cross stood there for a long moment, phone still in his hand, the silence heavy now. He knew exactly what this meant.

There would be no speeches.
No press conferences.
No applause.

Only files. Depositions. Motions filed minutes before deadlines. Judges forced to choose between the law and their careers.

He walked to his desk and opened the bottom drawer.

Inside was a single folder. Blank. Unlabeled.

He placed it on the desk and opened it anyway.

"This is how it starts," he said to the empty room.

Not with sirens.
Not with arrests.

With a lawyer deciding that this time, the law would not blink first.

End of Chapter One

Chapter Two

The Folder

Daniel Cross did not pack a suitcase.

He packed documents.

A passport. A spare phone. A legal pad. A pen that never failed. A small stack of crisp shirts he could fold without thinking. Everything else could be replaced.

He moved through his apartment in silence, not rushing, not hesitating. He did not turn on a light. He did not make coffee. He did not open the curtains.

He treated the morning like a deposition. Only facts. No emotion.

At 5:03 a.m., the elevator opened to the lobby. The doorman looked up and started to speak, then caught himself. Cross had that effect on people. He made them question whether their words were worth the air.

"Morning, Mr. Cross," the doorman said quietly.

Cross nodded once and walked out into the cold.

A black sedan waited at the curb. No markings. No plates that meant anything. The driver stepped out as Cross approached.

The driver was tall and broad, with a face built for blunt decisions. He wore a plain coat, gloves, and the kind of calm that only comes from training or regret.

"Mr. Cross," he said.

"Daniel," Cross replied.

The driver opened the back door.

Cross slid in. The interior smelled like leather and disinfectant. A faint hint of metal. The driver got in and pulled away without asking where.

For ten minutes they rode through sleeping streets. No radio. No talk. The car moved like it belonged to the dark.

Finally the driver spoke.

"My name is Harlan Pike."

Cross watched the reflections in the window, buildings smearing into black glass.

"I did not ask," Cross said.

"You would have eventually."

Cross glanced at him in the mirror. Pike did not flinch.

"Where are we going?" Cross asked.

Pike nodded once, as if he had been waiting for permission to answer.

"Federal building. Not the one with tourists. Not the one with flags. Another one."

Cross did not respond.

Pike continued anyway.

"They set up a room in the basement. No windows. No signage. If you do not know it exists, you will never find it."

"Who are they?" Cross asked.

Pike smiled, and it was not friendly.

"The people who are tired."

They turned onto a narrow street lined with service entrances and loading docks. A security gate slid open without the car stopping. They passed through a tunnel and emerged under concrete.

The sedan rolled into a parking bay lit by fluorescent hum. Two cameras rotated quietly. A single armed guard stood beside a steel door, eyes forward.

Pike killed the engine.

He looked back at Cross.

"One thing," Pike said. "Everything you say in that room can be used against you."

Cross stared at him.

"That is a joke," Pike added.

Cross opened the door and stepped out.

The air down there was stale and cold. The kind of air that never touched daylight. Cross adjusted his coat, then followed Pike toward the steel door.

The guard scanned Pike, then scanned Cross.

"Name," the guard said.

"Daniel Cross," Cross replied.

The guard looked at a clipboard and nodded. He did not smile. He did not offer a welcome.

The steel door opened with a heavy click.

Beyond it was a hallway with bare walls and a low ceiling. A security camera watched them pass. Another watched from the other direction. The lights were too bright and too constant, like interrogation lamps that never turned off.

They stopped at a second door. This one had no handle, only a keypad and a small black lens.

Pike leaned toward the lens.

"Package is here," Pike said.

A voice crackled through a speaker. Flat. Calm.

"Proceed."

The door unlocked.

Cross stepped into a room that was smaller than he expected. A long table. Six chairs. A screen mounted on the far wall. A file cabinet. A safe. A pot of coffee that looked like it had been left behind as a courtesy, not a comfort.

Four people were already seated.

They did not stand when he entered.

That told Cross everything.

The woman at the head of the table looked up first. Late forties. Clean suit. Hair pulled back tight. Eyes sharp enough to cut paper.

"Daniel Cross," she said.

He did not correct her for using his full name. In that room, names were weapons. They used the whole blade.

"Yes."

"My name is Elise Warren," she said. "You are going to treat this room like it does not exist."

Cross took a chair without asking.

He sat, placed his legal pad on the table, and waited.

Warren slid a folder across the table toward him.

It was thick. Heavier than paper. It looked like it contained years.

No label. No title. No agency stamp.

Cross opened it.

The first page was a list of numbers.

Not dates.
Not case citations.

Account numbers.

Below them were names of entities that looked harmless. Community initiatives. Child development partnerships. Health outreach coalitions. Transportation safety improvements.

Each name sounded like charity. Like help. Like the sort of thing no one wanted to question.

Cross flipped the page.

A map.

Not a political map. Not a tourist map.

A map of money.

Lines ran from state to state, from agencies to nonprofits, from nonprofits to contractors, from contractors to consulting firms, from consulting firms to accounts overseas.

Some lines ended in places everyone knew.

Some ended in places no one ever talked about.

Cross felt his pulse slow. That was his body's way of preparing.

Warren watched him like a prosecutor watching a witness.

"Tell me what you see," Warren said.

Cross tapped the page with the tip of his pen.

"I see a distribution network," he said. "Layered. Deliberate. Designed to look like oversight while hiding extraction."

One of the men on the far side of the table shifted in his chair. He looked young for this room, early thirties, with a tight jaw and a restless knee. He wore the plain suit of a government attorney who had never learned how to relax.

"You speak like you have seen it before," the man said.

Cross looked at him.

"I have," Cross replied. "Just not this big."

Warren leaned forward.

"It is bigger," she said. "And it is protected. This network is not stealing from one program. It is stealing from the idea that the programs matter."

Cross flipped another page.

He stopped.

Photographs.

A daycare building. Faded paint. A sign out front with a cheerful name and cartoon animals. Another photo showed an empty room with cots stacked against a wall.

The next photo showed a state grant approval letter with a signature.

The next photo showed a bank transfer receipt.

Then an image of a man shaking hands with a state official in front of a ribbon cutting.

Cross looked up.

"Why is this in here?" he asked.

Warren's face did not change.

"Because this is the lie," she said. "That daycare received three million dollars across two years for expansion and staffing. According to state reporting, it serves one hundred and twelve children."

"And?" Cross asked.

Warren slid another page toward him.

It was a report. A surprise inspection.

Cross read the first line.

No children present.

He read the next line.

No staff present.

He read the next.

No operational evidence.

Cross kept reading, and the feeling in his stomach changed from interest to anger.

The young man at the table spoke again.

"That daycare exists on paper," he said. "The building is real. The service is not. The money went out anyway."

Cross looked back at the map.

"How many?" Cross asked.

Warren did not answer immediately.

Instead she reached into her briefcase and set a flash drive on the table.

Cross did not touch it.

Warren nodded at the drive.

"That is the first cut. Fifty-seven entities across eleven states. We believe there are more. We believe it branches into medical billing and transportation contracts. We believe it routes into foreign accounts through shell foundations."

Cross stared at the drive.

"And you want me to do what?" he asked.

Warren held his gaze.

"We want you to build the case that does not collapse," she said. "We want you to pick the first domino and push it so hard the rest cannot pretend they are not connected."

Cross felt the room tighten around the question.

The quiet in that basement was not silence. It was pressure.

He closed the folder carefully and set it down.

"You know what happens when you push the first domino," Cross said.

Warren nodded.

"They will come for the person who pushed it," she said.

Cross looked at each face around the table. They all carried the same expression. Not fear. Not excitement.

Commitment.

Cross spoke softly.

"Who authorized this?" he asked.

Warren's eyes did not blink.

"The highest level you can imagine," she said. "And a few levels you cannot."

Cross leaned back in his chair.

He did not smile.

He did not laugh.

He only asked the question that mattered.

"Who is dirty in this room?" he said.

No one moved.

No one answered.

That was the first answer.

Warren reached into the folder and pulled out one last page. She slid it toward him.

A single name was typed at the top.

A judge.

Not just any judge.

A federal judge.

Cross felt the temperature in the room drop.

Warren spoke carefully now, like she was placing a loaded weapon on the table.

"He has been stopping cases quietly," she said. "He does not dismiss them. He delays them. He buries them in procedure. He forces settlements. He drains agencies until they walk away."

Cross stared at the name.

"And you want me to indict the system," Cross said.

Warren's voice was steady.

"We want you to indict the part of the system that thinks it is untouchable."

Cross looked down at the name again.

Then he wrote a single word on his legal pad.

Start.

He slid the pad forward so Warren could see it.

"Then we do it right," Cross said. "And we do it fast."

Warren nodded once.

"Good," she said. "Because they already know you are here."

Cross froze.

"Who?" he asked.

Warren did not answer with a name.

She answered with a fact.

"The first leak came in before you walked through the door."

End of Chapter Two

Chapter Three

The Leak

Daniel Cross had learned long ago that leaks did not happen by accident.

They were decisions. Calculated. Timed. Made by people who believed they would never be exposed.

He closed the folder and pushed it back toward Elise Warren.

"Who knows my name is attached to this," Cross asked.

Warren folded her hands on the table.

"Officially?" she said. "No one."

"Unofficially?"

She glanced toward the others. The young attorney looked down. The older man with silver hair kept his eyes on the table. The fourth member, a woman with a scar along her jawline, met Cross's gaze without blinking.

Warren answered.

"At least one federal agency. At least two state offices. And someone inside the judiciary."

Cross nodded slowly.

"That narrows nothing," he said.

"It narrows everything," Warren replied. "Because they are already reacting."

Cross stood and walked to the screen mounted on the wall.

"Turn it on," he said.

No one questioned him. The screen came alive.

A news feed appeared. Not national. Regional. A legal blog Cross recognized. The kind that prosecutors pretended not to read but always did.

The headline was small but sharp.

UNNAMED TASK FORCE TARGETS MULTI STATE GRANT FRAUD

Cross felt the familiar tightening behind his eyes.

"They do not know the scope," he said. "That means the leak came from someone close enough to see movement, but far enough away to guess."

The scarred woman spoke for the first time.

"Transportation office," she said. "Midwest. We pulled records last week."

Cross turned to her.

"They noticed?" he asked.

"They always notice," she said. "They just pretend not to."

Cross studied the headline again.

"Who benefits from panic right now?" he asked.

The young attorney answered too quickly.

"Everyone who is guilty."

Cross shook his head.

"No," he said. "Everyone who wants to control the narrative."

He turned back to Warren.

"They will try to frame this as overreach," Cross said. "A fishing expedition. Political theater. They will push judges to demand names and timelines before we are ready."

Warren nodded.

"They already have," she said. "Two emergency motions were filed overnight."

Cross smiled faintly.

"Good," he said. "That means they are afraid."

He returned to his seat and opened his legal pad.

"Show me the weakest link," he said.

Warren hesitated.

"That is not how we planned this," she said.

Cross looked up.

"Plans are for people who believe the other side will follow rules," he said. "They will not. We need a case that looks small enough to ignore and strong enough to survive."

The scarred woman slid a thin file across the table.

"This one," she said. "A regional medical transport contract. Non emergency services. The numbers are inflated but the paperwork is sloppy."

Cross flipped through the pages.

Billing codes. Mileage logs. Driver rosters.

He stopped at a signature.

"This person signs too much," Cross said.

"He signs everything," the young attorney said. "Because he thinks volume equals invisibility."

Cross tapped the page.

"This is our door," Cross said. "Not the building. The door."

Warren frowned.

"It only touches one state," she said.

Cross looked at her.

"Indictments do not start with explosions," he said. "They start with cracks."

He wrote a name on the legal pad.

"Who is this?" Cross asked.

The silver haired man finally spoke.

"A deputy director," he said. "Career. No public profile. Well connected."

"Good," Cross said. "He will fold."

Warren leaned forward.

"You do not know that," she said.

Cross met her eyes.

"I know the type," he said. "He believes the system will protect him. When it does not, he will trade everything for survival."

The screen on the wall changed.

Another alert.

STATE OFFICIAL DENIES KNOWLEDGE OF FRAUD INVESTIGATION

Cross watched the words scroll.

"They are moving faster," he said. "We need to move first."

Warren exhaled slowly.

"What are you proposing?" she asked.

Cross closed his legal pad.

"We file a sealed indictment," he said. "Limited scope. Narrow charges. Clean facts. No speeches."

The young attorney looked startled.

"That will trigger discovery," he said.

"Yes," Cross replied. "And discovery is where people make mistakes."

Warren considered him carefully.

"You realize once we file, we cannot stop," she said.

Cross stood.

"That is the point."

The room fell silent again. Not tense. Focused.

The scarred woman nodded once.

"I can have affidavits ready by noon," she said.

"Good," Cross said.

The silver haired man spoke.

"The judge?" he asked.

Cross did not hesitate.

"We do not give it to him," Cross said. "We file in a different district."

Warren's eyes widened.

"That will be seen as aggressive," she said.

Cross shrugged.

"They already called it that," he said.

He walked toward the door, then stopped.

"One more thing," Cross said.

They all looked at him.

"From this moment on," Cross said, "assume every call is recorded, every email is copied, and every silence is being interpreted."

He opened the door.

"And if anyone in this room is compromised," Cross added, "now is the last safe moment to walk away."

No one moved.

Cross nodded.

"Then let us teach them something," he said. "The law still works when someone is willing to use it."

He stepped into the hallway.

Behind him, the screen refreshed again.

This time the headline was larger.

FEDERAL PROSECUTOR NAMED IN EXPANDING FRAUD PROBE

They had his name now.

Cross smiled to himself as the door closed.

Good.

Fear made people sloppy.

And sloppy was how empires fell.

End of Chapter Three

Chapter Four

The First Domino

The courthouse did not look like a place where history began.

It looked tired.

Daniel Cross walked through the side entrance just after noon, coat buttoned, face neutral, carrying a thin briefcase that suggested routine business. That was intentional. Power did not announce itself. It slipped in quietly and took a seat.

Inside, the air smelled faintly of disinfectant and old paper. The security guard glanced at Cross's credentials and waved him through without comment.

Courtroom 3B sat at the end of a narrow hallway. No reporters. No cameras. No protestors. Just a clerk shuffling papers and a bailiff leaning against the wall like this was any other afternoon.

That was exactly how Cross wanted it.

He entered and took his place at the table on the left. Across from him, the defense attorney flipped through a file and avoided eye contact. A man in his late fifties sat beside the attorney, shoulders stiff, hands clasped so tightly his knuckles had gone pale.

The deputy director.

He looked smaller in person.

The judge entered without ceremony. A different judge. Younger. Careful. The kind who read everything twice and spoke once.

"Be seated," the judge said.

Cross remained standing just long enough to be noticed.

"Your Honor," Cross said. "Daniel Cross for the United States."

The judge glanced at him, then down at the docket.

"I was not expecting you, Mr. Cross," the judge said.

"That is usually the case," Cross replied.

The defense attorney cleared his throat.

"Your Honor, before we proceed, I must object to the presence of Mr. Cross. His involvement suggests—"

Cross cut him off gently.

"Suggests nothing," Cross said. "It confirms jurisdiction."

The judge raised a hand.

"Counsel," the judge said, "you will have your turn."

The defense attorney sat back, displeased.

Cross opened his briefcase and removed a single document. He placed it on the table and slid it forward.

"We are here on a sealed indictment," Cross said. "Limited charges. Financial fraud. False statements. Conspiracy."

The deputy director shifted in his chair.

The judge adjusted his glasses.

"I see the seal," the judge said. "Why here?"

"Because the conduct occurred here," Cross said. "And because the evidence survives scrutiny."

The judge studied Cross carefully.

"You understand the implications," the judge said.

"Yes," Cross replied.

"Very well," the judge said. "Proceed."

Cross stood.

He did not pace. He did not raise his voice. He spoke like a man reciting facts to himself.

"Over a period of eighteen months," Cross said, "the defendant approved and authorized payment requests for medical transport services that were never rendered, at rates that exceeded contractual limits, supported by documentation he knew to be false."

The defense attorney stood.

"Objection," he said. "Speculation."

Cross turned slightly.

"Every statement I just made is supported by sworn affidavits, billing records, GPS data, and internal emails authored by your client," Cross said.

The attorney opened his mouth again.

The judge raised a finger.

"Sit down," the judge said.

The deputy director swallowed.

Cross continued.

"These payments were routed through a third party contractor," Cross said. "That contractor transferred funds to a consulting entity. That entity then distributed money to accounts controlled by individuals who had no legitimate business relationship to the program."

Cross paused.

"The defendant signed every approval himself."

The judge leaned forward.

"And your theory is that he acted alone," the judge said.

Cross shook his head once.

"No," Cross said. "Our theory is that he acted first."

The room felt smaller.

The defense attorney spoke again, his voice tight.

"Your Honor, this is an attempt to turn a bureaucratic oversight issue into a criminal case."

Cross smiled faintly.

"If this were oversight," Cross said, "we would not be here."

He turned to the judge.

"Your Honor," Cross said, "we are asking the court to unseal counts one through three and remand the defendant pending further proceedings."

The judge studied the defendant. A man who had believed his position insulated him from consequence.

"Counsel," the judge said to the defense attorney, "do you have anything substantive to add?"

The attorney hesitated.

"No," he said quietly.

The judge nodded.

"So ordered," the judge said.

The sound of the gavel was sharp and final.

The bailiff moved toward the defendant.

"Sir," the bailiff said, "please stand."

The deputy director's chair scraped against the floor.

As he was led away, his eyes met Cross's.

There was no anger there.

Only realization.

Cross packed his briefcase and walked out without looking back.

Outside, his phone vibrated.

One message.

UNKNOWN NUMBER: They will come faster now.

Cross typed a response.

CROSS: That was always the plan.

He slipped the phone back into his pocket and stepped into the sunlight.

Behind him, a small case had been unsealed.

In offices across the country, phones began to ring.

Emails were forwarded.

Documents were deleted too late.

The first domino had fallen.

And the rest of them were already leaning.

End of Chapter Four

Chapter Five

Pressure

By nightfall, everyone who mattered knew.

Daniel Cross stood in a borrowed office three floors above the street, lights off, watching the city glow through the glass. Phones moved like nervous insects in office towers across town. Conversations stopped when doors opened. Names were spoken carefully now.

That was the first real effect of an indictment.
Not fear.
Pressure.

His phone rang.

This time, the number was not blocked.

"Cross," he said.

"You filed in the wrong district."

The voice was smooth. Older. Used to being obeyed.

Cross did not turn from the window.

"There is no wrong district," Cross said. "Only jurisdiction and evidence."

A quiet breath on the other end.

"You are forcing hands," the voice said.

"I am testing integrity," Cross replied.

Another pause.

"You think this ends with a deputy director?" the voice asked.

Cross smiled faintly.

"No," he said. "I think this starts with one."

The call ended without goodbye.

Cross set the phone down and opened a new folder. This one already had tabs. Medical. Transportation. Grants. Oversight.

He flipped to the first page in Medical.

A spreadsheet filled the screen. Billing codes repeated too cleanly. Numbers rounded where they should not be. Patterns no one noticed because no one wanted to.

A knock came at the door.

"Come in," Cross said.

Elise Warren stepped inside, coat still on, eyes sharp.

"They are scrambling," she said. "Two states froze payments within an hour. Three agencies issued internal memos telling staff not to speak to anyone."

Cross nodded.

"Silence is a confession when it is sudden," he said.

Warren walked closer.

"There is a problem," she said.

Cross waited.

"The judge," Warren said. "The one we flagged. He issued a standing order this afternoon. Any case involving federal grant fraud now requires additional review."

Cross turned to face her.

"In his courtroom," Cross said.

"Yes."

Cross considered that.

"He wants control," Cross said. "And visibility."

"He wants leverage," Warren corrected.

Cross nodded.

"Then we deny him both," Cross said.

Warren folded her arms.

"How?" she asked.

Cross slid a document across the desk.

"A second indictment," Cross said. "Different state. Different scheme. Different judge."

Warren glanced at the page.

"This is aggressive," she said.

"This is insulation," Cross replied.

Her phone buzzed. She glanced at it, then looked up.

"You have been requested upstairs," she said.

Cross raised an eyebrow.

"By?" he asked.

Warren hesitated.

"By people who do not usually request," she said.

Cross closed the folder.

"Good," he said. "It means the pressure is working."

They walked together to the elevator.

Inside, the doors closed with a soft thud. The ride up was silent.

When the doors opened, two men waited. Suits. Pins. Credentials visible but unnecessary.

"Mr. Cross," one of them said. "We would like a word."

Cross nodded once.

They led him into a conference room with a long table and a single file in the center.

"This case is getting attention," the man said.

"It should," Cross replied.

The second man leaned forward.

"You are creating instability," he said.

Cross met his eyes.

"I am exposing it," Cross said. "Instability was already there."

The first man opened the file.

"There are concerns," he said. "About scope. About tone."

Cross did not look at the file.

"Concern is the currency of people who waited too long," Cross said.

Silence followed.

Then the first man spoke again.

"What do you want?" he asked.

Cross answered without hesitation.

"Time," Cross said. "And distance."

"For what?" the second man asked.

"For the law to do its job," Cross said.

The men exchanged a glance.

"We cannot guarantee protection," the first man said.

Cross stood.

"I did not ask for it," he said.

He walked out without waiting for dismissal.

Back downstairs, Warren was waiting.

"They tried to slow you," she said.

"They failed," Cross replied.

Outside, night had fully settled. The city buzzed with rumors now, half truths layered over fear.

Cross's phone vibrated again.

This time it was a text.

UNKNOWN NUMBER: We can make this easier.

Cross typed back.

CROSS: Then tell the truth.

The reply took longer.

UNKNOWN NUMBER: We need assurances.

Cross stared at the screen.

CROSS: The law does not offer comfort. Only outcomes.

He put the phone away.

Across the country, a man sat in a quiet office staring at his own reflection, weighing loyalty against survival.

The pressure was doing its work.

And soon, someone would crack.

End of Chapter Five

Chapter Six

The First Crack

The man waited until after midnight.

That was when he felt safest. When offices were dark, phones unanswered, and decisions felt smaller because no one was watching. He sat alone at his kitchen table with a glass of water he had not touched and a folder he had not opened.

His hands trembled anyway.

The phone vibrated once.

UNKNOWN NUMBER: We need to talk.

He stared at the screen. He knew better than to reply with words.

He typed a number.

UNKNOWN NUMBER: Where?

The reply came quickly.

CROSS: You choose. Quiet. Public enough to feel safe.

Ten minutes passed. Then fifteen.

UNKNOWN NUMBER: Parking garage. River Street. Top level.

Daniel Cross arrived early.

He parked two spaces away from the lone sedan already there. He did not approach immediately. He stood beside his car, letting the night settle, letting the other man feel the wait.

Finally the sedan door opened.

The man stepped out. Mid forties. Expensive coat. Nervous eyes. He looked like someone who had practiced confidence and recently lost it.

"You came alone," the man said.

"So did you," Cross replied.

They stood under a flickering light. The city hummed far below.

"I do not have much time," the man said.

"You have less than you think," Cross replied.

The man swallowed.

"They are blaming me," he said. "They say I signed off too much. That I should have asked questions."

"You should have," Cross said calmly.

The man flinched.

"They promised oversight," the man said. "They said the paperwork was clean."

Cross tilted his head slightly.

"Who is they?" Cross asked.

The man looked toward the edge of the garage, as if names might be written there.

"I want protection," the man said. "I want assurances."

Cross stepped closer. Not threatening. Certain.

"The only protection I offer is truth," Cross said. "And the only assurance is evidence."

The man laughed weakly.

"You cannot protect me," he said.

"No," Cross agreed. "But I can make sure you are not alone."

Silence stretched between them.

Finally, the man reached into his coat and pulled out a flash drive.

"I copied everything," he said. "Emails. Approvals. Side letters. Payment instructions that never went through official channels."

Cross did not take it yet.

"Why now?" Cross asked.

The man's voice dropped.

"Because they stopped returning my calls," he said.

Cross nodded.

"That is always the moment," Cross said.

He took the flash drive and slipped it into his pocket.

"Who else knows you are here?" Cross asked.

"No one," the man said too quickly.

Cross met his eyes.

"Try again," Cross said.

The man's shoulders slumped.

"One person," he said. "Judicial liaison. State level. He told me to wait. To stay quiet."

Cross felt the weight of the night press closer.

"Name," Cross said.

The man gave it.

Cross repeated it once, committing it to memory.

"Go home," Cross said. "Do not answer your phone. Do not delete anything. When they call, let it ring."

"And then?" the man asked.

Cross turned back toward his car.

"Then you tell the truth under oath," Cross said. "Or the truth will tell itself."

The man watched him leave.

Inside his borrowed office an hour later, Cross plugged the drive into a secured laptop.

Files bloomed across the screen.

There were more than he expected.

Payment schedules. Internal memos. Draft responses to audits that were never sent. A chain of messages with subject lines marked urgent.

One file caught his eye.

Judicial Review Coordination.

Cross opened it.

The name appeared again.

Same judge. Different context.

This was not delay. This was design.

Cross leaned back and closed his eyes for a moment.

When he opened them, he dialed Warren.

"We have our crack," Cross said.

"How bad?" she asked.

"Structural," Cross replied. "It touches the bench."

She was quiet.

"Send it," she said.

Cross forwarded the files.

Then he opened a new document.

Title: Indictment Two.

Outside, a janitor pushed a cart down the hallway, unaware that a quiet decision had just moved closer to daylight.

Across the country, a judge sat awake at his desk, staring at a sealed email he had not yet opened.

He hesitated.

That hesitation would cost him everything.

End of Chapter Six

Chapter Seven

The Judge

The judge had not slept.

He sat alone in his chambers, jacket folded over the back of the chair, tie loosened but not removed. He believed in appearances, even when no one was there to see them.

The email sat unopened on his screen.

Sealed.
Restricted.
Read receipt enabled.

He knew what it was without clicking.

For twenty years, he had built a reputation on restraint. Careful rulings. Thoughtful delays. Opinions that sounded balanced while quietly guiding outcomes. He told himself it was stewardship. That he was protecting institutions from reckless prosecutors and political pressure.

That story had served him well.

Until now.

He opened the email.

The first attachment loaded slowly, as if it wanted him to think twice.

He did not.

A spreadsheet appeared. Familiar formatting. Internal codes. He recognized them instantly because he had asked for them himself years earlier, framed as curiosity, framed as oversight.

He scrolled.

His name appeared once.

Then again.

Not in the way he preferred. Not in footnotes or calendars. In messages. Instructions.

Suggestions written carefully enough to pass as advice.

He felt a cold weight settle in his chest.

His phone rang.

He did not answer.

It rang again.

Still nothing.

The third time, he picked up.

"This is a mistake," he said before the other voice could speak.

"Then you should welcome the review," the voice replied.

It was calm. Younger. Not someone he recognized.

"You do not understand," the judge said. "There are processes."

"Yes," the voice said. "And you have been managing them."

The judge stood and paced.

"You cannot prove intent," he said. "Delays are not crimes."

The voice did not argue.

"No," it said. "But coordination is."

The call ended.

The judge stared at the phone like it had betrayed him.

Down the hall, his clerk worked late, unaware that the man she trusted was watching his world narrow to a single point.

Across town, Daniel Cross read through the final file twice.

Once for facts.
Once for motive.

He did not rush.

When he finished, he closed the laptop and leaned back.

"This is it," Warren said from the doorway.

Cross nodded.

"He did not take money," Cross said. "That is what he told himself."

"But he took influence," Warren replied.

"And protection," Cross added.

Warren stepped inside.

"He is calling people," she said. "Trying to figure out how exposed he is."

Cross smiled faintly.

"That means he already knows," Cross said.

Warren crossed her arms.

"If we name him," she said, "everything explodes."

Cross met her eyes.

"That is what happens when the truth hits oxygen," he said.

She hesitated.

"Once we file, there is no unfiling," she said.

Cross turned back to the screen.

"Then we do not flinch," he said.

He opened Indictment Two and added a paragraph.

Judicial interference.
Conspiracy to obstruct federal investigations.
Abuse of authority.

He saved the document.

At the courthouse, the judge opened a drawer and removed a thick envelope.

Inside were handwritten notes he had never destroyed. Reminders. Connections. Names he never thought would matter again.

He stared at them.

Then he closed the drawer without taking them.

That choice would haunt him.

Cross stood and put on his coat.

"Where are you going?" Warren asked.

"To file," Cross said.

Outside, dawn crept across the sky, pale and indifferent.

Somewhere between night and morning, a line had been crossed.

By noon, the country would know.

And by nightfall, nothing would be the same.

End of Chapter Seven

Chapter Eight

Exposure

The clerk read the filing twice.

Not because it was unclear. Because it was unprecedented.

She sat behind the counter in a quiet federal office where days blurred together and filings rarely surprised her. This one did. The caption alone made her pause. The allegations inside made her throat tighten.

She stamped it.

That sound echoed farther than she knew.

By the time Daniel Cross reached the street, the document was already moving. Digitized. Replicated. Logged into systems that did not forget. The seal held, but seals only delayed truth. They never stopped it.

His phone vibrated before he reached the car.

WARREN: It is live.

CROSS: Then we wait.

WARREN: They will not.

Cross slid into the driver's seat and pulled away from the curb. Traffic had thickened. Morning commuters, unaware that something fundamental had shifted while they slept.

At the courthouse, the judge's clerk noticed the alert first.

She frowned at her screen, refreshed it, then checked the docket again. Her stomach dropped.

She stood and knocked on the chamber door.

"Judge," she said carefully. "There is a new filing."

No answer.

She knocked again, louder.

Still nothing.

Inside the chamber, the judge sat perfectly still, hands folded on the desk, eyes fixed on the wall. He had already seen it. A courtesy text had arrived minutes earlier from someone who no longer returned his calls.

Filed.
Named.
Unavoidable.

He stood and straightened his jacket.

For the first time in years, he felt the law standing across from him instead of beneath him.

Across the city, a conference room filled with voices.

"They crossed a line," one man said.

"They crossed several," another replied.

A third voice cut through the noise.

"They crossed ours."

Phones buzzed. Screens lit up. Assistants moved quickly now, carrying binders and whispering names.

"Find out who else is exposed," someone ordered.

"Freeze communications," another said.

"Get ahead of the press," a third insisted.

But the press was already circling.

A legal correspondent refreshed her feed and leaned forward.

"That cannot be right," she murmured.

She checked again.

It was right.

Her editor walked by.

"Anything?" he asked.

She turned her screen toward him.

He stopped walking.

"We need confirmation," he said.

She nodded, fingers already moving.

CONFIRMATION REQUEST SENT.

The reply came faster than expected.

NO COMMENT AT THIS TIME.

The editor smiled grimly.

"That is confirmation," he said.

Daniel Cross parked in a public garage and sat for a moment with the engine off. He breathed once, slow and measured.

Then his phone rang.

This time, the number was familiar.

"You filed," the voice said.

"Yes," Cross replied.

"You named him."

"Yes."

"You realize what this does," the voice said.

Cross looked straight ahead.

"It tells the truth," Cross said.

Silence followed.

"You will be blamed for what comes next," the voice said.

Cross considered that.

"People blame storms for rain," Cross said. "Not the clouds that built them."

The line went dead.

Across the country, servers strained under sudden traffic. Quiet filings became trending searches. Law firms held emergency meetings. Compliance officers stared at spreadsheets they had ignored for years.

In one small office, the man from the parking garage watched the news with shaking hands.

"They did it," he whispered.

In another office, a different man deleted an email and immediately regretted it.

At the courthouse, the judge's clerk sat at her desk, staring at the door to chambers, wondering how something that felt so permanent could unravel so quickly.

By noon, the first headline broke.

FEDERAL INDICTMENT NAMES SITTING JUDGE IN EXPANDING FRAUD CASE

Daniel Cross read it once and set the phone down.

This was no longer a case.

It was a reckoning.

And the system had just realized it could be named.

End of Chapter Eight

Chapter Nine

Counterstrike

The response was immediate.

Not public. Not official.
Private. Coordinated. Ruthless.

Daniel Cross felt it before he saw it.

His access badge failed at the garage gate.

The red light blinked once, then stayed solid.

Cross did not try again. He reversed, parked on the street, and walked the remaining block. Small disruptions always came first. They were tests. If you complained, they learned something. If you adapted, they learned more.

Inside the building, Warren was already waiting.

"They are pushing back," she said.

Cross nodded.

"They always do after exposure," he said. "Show me how."

Warren handed him a tablet.

Three motions had been filed overnight. Emergency relief. Jurisdictional challenge. Allegations of prosecutorial misconduct.

Cross scanned them quickly.

"They are not trying to win," Cross said.

"They are trying to slow," Warren replied.

"And divide," Cross added.

He handed the tablet back.

"They will go after credibility next," Cross said. "Mine. Yours. Anyone who touched this."

As if summoned, Cross's phone vibrated.

MEDIA REQUEST: Allegations of political motive. Response?

Cross showed Warren the screen.

"Here it is," he said.

Warren exhaled.

"They want you to speak," she said.

"They want me to slip," Cross replied.

He typed a response.

NO COMMENT. THE FILING SPEAKS FOR ITSELF.

He put the phone down.

Across town, a different meeting was underway.

The room was windowless. Phones sat face down. No notes were taken.

"He named a judge," one man said. "That breaks the rules."

"Those rules protected us," another replied.

A third voice spoke quietly.

"The rules only work if everyone obeys them."

Silence followed.

Then the first man leaned forward.

"Find something on him," he said. "Anything."

At the courthouse, the judge's attorney reviewed the indictment line by line. Each sentence felt heavier than the last.

"This is not political," the attorney said finally. "It is surgical."

The judge stared at the wall.

"Can we fight it?" he asked.

The attorney hesitated.

"We can challenge procedure," he said. "But the evidence is deep."

The judge closed his eyes.

"Then delay," he said.

"We will try," the attorney replied.

Back in his office, Cross opened a secure message.

FROM: Unknown
CONTENT: You are making enemies you cannot defeat.

Cross typed back without pause.

CROSS: I am naming them.

The reply took longer this time.

FROM: Unknown
CONTENT: This ends badly.

Cross stared at the screen, then locked the phone.

Warren watched him.

"They are afraid now," she said.

"No," Cross replied. "They are desperate. Fear comes later."

He pulled a new file from his drawer.

"What is that?" Warren asked.

"Transportation," Cross said. "Second layer."

She frowned.

"That touches five states," she said.

"Yes," Cross replied. "Which means five chances for someone to flip."

Warren studied him.

"They will accuse you of escalation," she said.

Cross looked up.

"Escalation is what happens when lies run out of room," he said.

Outside, sirens echoed faintly. Somewhere a reporter rehearsed a question. Somewhere an official rehearsed a denial.

Inside the system, fault lines widened.

By evening, another headline appeared.

MULTIPLE STATES CONFIRM FEDERAL INQUIRIES INTO TRANSPORT CONTRACTS

Daniel Cross read it once and closed the browser.

The counterstrike had begun.

So had the collapse.

End of Chapter Nine

Chapter Ten

The Testimony

The man asked for a lawyer before he asked for water.

That told Daniel Cross everything.

They sat in a small interview room with beige walls and a table bolted to the floor. A camera watched from the corner, red light steady. The clock on the wall ticked louder than it should have.

The witness was mid level. Important enough to know things. Replaceable enough to sacrifice.

He kept his hands folded, posture stiff, eyes darting toward the door every few seconds.

"State your name for the record," Cross said.

The man did.

"Do you understand why you are here?" Cross asked.

The man nodded.

"My attorney said you have questions," he replied.

Cross glanced at the attorney, who sat silent and alert.

"We have answers," Cross said. "What we are waiting on is honesty."

The man swallowed.

"I did not steal anything," he said.

Cross did not argue.

"I believe you," Cross said.

The man looked surprised.

Cross leaned forward slightly.

"You approved things," Cross continued. "You forwarded things. You assumed oversight existed somewhere else."

The man's shoulders sagged.

"They told me it was reviewed," he said. "That it had already been cleared."

"By who?" Cross asked.

The man hesitated.

"Names," Cross said calmly.

The man closed his eyes.

He spoke the first name.

Then another.

Then a third.

The attorney shifted in his chair.

Cross wrote nothing. He let the silence do the work.

"And the transportation contracts," Cross said finally.

The man shook his head.

"I never saw the end recipients," he said. "Only the front entities."

Cross nodded.

"That is how distance is created," Cross said. "Who told you not to look further?"

The man hesitated longer this time.

"An advisor," he said. "He said it was sensitive."

Cross glanced at the attorney.

"That advisor is not present," Cross said. "And he will not be protecting you."

The man's breathing quickened.

"They said this was normal," he said. "That everyone did it."

Cross met his eyes.

"Everyone lies until someone is sworn," Cross said.

The man stared at the table.

"I will cooperate," he said quietly.

Cross nodded once.

"Good," Cross said. "Then we begin."

Hours later, Cross stepped into the hallway and closed the door behind him. Warren waited nearby, arms crossed, eyes sharp.

"He flipped," she said.

"He leaned," Cross replied. "He will flip again."

She smiled faintly.

"What did he give you?" she asked.

Cross handed her a notepad with a single phrase written on it.

Central coordination office.

Warren read it twice.

"That does not officially exist," she said.

Cross nodded.

"That is why it matters," he said.

Her phone buzzed.

She read the message and looked up.

"Transportation just froze another state," she said. "And a medical board issued a quiet resignation."

Cross exhaled slowly.

"The pressure is spreading," he said.

Across the city, a conference call dissolved into shouting.

"They are talking," one voice said.

"Who?" another demanded.

"Everyone," came the reply.

In a quiet house far from Washington, a woman stared at her laptop, fingers hovering over the keyboard. She had been careful for years. Careful enough to believe she would never be noticed.

She began to type an email.

Back in his office, Cross opened a new folder.

Witness Statements.

He placed the first transcript inside.

Ten minutes later, his phone vibrated.

UNKNOWN NUMBER: We need to discuss terms.

Cross did not smile.

He typed one word.

CROSS: Good.

He set the phone down and looked out at the city.

The case was no longer about exposure.

It was about testimony.

And testimony, once given, never went back.

Chapter Eleven

The Offer

The email arrived just before dawn.

No subject line.
No signature.
Just a meeting request and a location.

Daniel Cross read it once, then deleted it without responding.

Ten seconds later, his phone rang.

"You got the message," the voice said.

"Yes," Cross replied.

"You did not reply."

"No," Cross said.

A short pause.

"This is not how negotiations usually work," the voice said.

Cross leaned back in his chair.

"That is because this is not a negotiation," Cross said.

Silence stretched.

"People above you are concerned," the voice said carefully.

Cross smiled faintly.

"People above me have been concerned for a while," he said.

"You are destabilizing systems," the voice continued. "There are consequences."

"There were consequences before I arrived," Cross replied. "They were just hidden."

Another pause.

"We can make this end cleanly," the voice said. "Focused indictments. Limited fallout. You keep your reputation."

Cross closed his eyes briefly.

"Tell me what you want," he said.

Relief slipped into the voice.

"The judge," it said. "We want him separated from the rest."

Cross opened his eyes.

"No," he said.

"You are protecting larger actors," the voice pressed. "This is triage."

Cross stood and walked to the window.

"Triage saves lives," Cross said. "This saves careers."

The voice hardened.

"You are not as insulated as you think," it said.

Cross lowered his voice.

"Threats confirm guilt," he said. "And they are recorded."

The call ended abruptly.

Warren appeared in the doorway moments later.

"They reached out," she said.

"Yes," Cross replied.

"What did they offer?" she asked.

Cross turned.

"Silence," he said.

Warren exhaled.

"They will escalate," she said.

"They already are," Cross replied.

He handed her a folder.

"What is this?" she asked.

"Witness Eleven," Cross said. "Transportation. Senior level."

Warren's eyebrows rose.

"They are lining up," she said.

"They are panicking," Cross corrected.

Across the city, the judge sat in his attorney's office, hands clasped, listening.

"They want to isolate you," the attorney said. "Make you the storm wall."

The judge stared at the carpet.

"Can we survive it?" he asked.

The attorney hesitated.

"Only if others stay silent," he said.

The judge closed his eyes.

Elsewhere, a woman pressed send on an email she had drafted for hours.

It went to Daniel Cross.

SUBJECT: I HAVE DOCUMENTS

Cross read it once.

Then again.

He forwarded it to Warren with a single line.

CROSS: This one is big.

Warren looked up slowly.

"How big?" she asked.

Cross met her eyes.

"Big enough that they will stop asking and start begging," he said.

Outside, the sun rose over a country that had no idea how close it was to seeing itself clearly.

And somewhere deep inside the system, the offer turned into a warning.

Which meant the end was getting closer.

End of Chapter Eleven

Chapter Twelve

The Documents

The woman arrived alone.

That alone told Daniel Cross more than any résumé ever could.

She walked into the federal building just after noon carrying a plain leather tote, the kind sold in airport shops and forgotten easily. She did not look nervous. She looked resolved. There was a difference.

Warren met her first.

"I am Elise Warren," she said. "You asked to see Mr. Cross."

"I know," the woman replied. "And yes."

They escorted her to a small conference room with no windows and a single camera mounted high in the corner. Cross stood when she entered.

"Thank you for coming," he said.

She nodded and set the tote on the table.

"My name does not matter," she said. "Not yet."

Cross did not argue.

"That bag does," he replied.

She opened it.

Inside were folders. Color coded. Labeled by year. By program. By state.

Warren felt her breath catch.

"You kept everything," Warren said.

"I was told to," the woman replied. "At first."

Cross picked up one folder and opened it carefully.

Email chains. Approval memos. Side agreements. Notes written in the margins of official forms.

He stopped at one page.

A directive.

Not signed. Not letterheaded.

But unmistakable.

"Where did this come from?" Cross asked.

The woman met his eyes.

"The central coordination office," she said. "The one they say does not exist."

Cross closed the folder slowly.

"How long?" he asked.

"Seven years," she replied. "Longer if you count the pilot phase."

Warren sat down.

"This is nationwide," she said.

"Yes," the woman replied. "And international."

Cross felt the room tighten.

"Explain," he said.

The woman inhaled once.

"Funds were routed through domestic programs into partner organizations overseas," she said. "They called it humanitarian alignment. Development assistance. Oversight was fictional."

She slid a document forward.

"These are the foreign accounts," she said. "These are the intermediaries. These are the return channels."

Cross scanned the page.

"Political insulation," he said quietly.

The woman nodded.

"They told us it was untouchable," she said. "That it was too big."

"Why come forward now?" Warren asked.

The woman's jaw tightened.

"Because they started destroying records," she said. "And because they told me to lie."

Cross looked at her.

"Who?" he asked.

She gave a name.

Warren stiffened.

"That puts us past the point of containment," Warren said.

Cross nodded.

"Yes," he said. "It does."

He looked back at the woman.

"You understand what happens next," Cross said.

"I do," she replied. "I am ready."

Cross slid a form across the table.

"Then we begin the record," he said.

Hours later, the tote was empty and the table was covered.

The scope was undeniable now.

Not corruption at the edges.
Architecture at the center.

Cross closed the last folder and leaned back.

"This changes everything," Warren said.

"It clarifies everything," Cross replied.

Across the city, a secure call connected three offices.

"They have documents," one voice said.

"How many?" another asked.

"Enough," came the reply.

A third voice spoke softly.

"Then it is no longer about stopping him," it said. "It is about surviving."

Back in the conference room, Cross stood.

"Get these digitized," he said. "Redundant storage. Independent review."

Warren nodded.

"And Cross," she said.

"Yes?"

"They are going to try to discredit her," Warren said.

Cross looked at the closed door.

"They will fail," he said. "Truth ages better than lies."

Outside, the building hummed with ordinary work.

Inside, a case crossed the threshold from dangerous to unstoppable.

End of Chapter Twelve

Chapter Thirteen

The Hearing

The courtroom was full before anyone admitted it mattered.

No cameras were allowed, but everyone knew the doors would not stay closed for long. Attorneys filled the benches. Observers pretended not to observe. Federal marshals stood a little straighter than usual.

Daniel Cross sat at the government table with a single binder.

Across from him, the defense had three.

The judge entered and took the bench without looking at either side.

"Be seated," the judge said.

The room settled, but the tension did not.

"We are here on multiple motions," the judge continued. "Jurisdiction, scope, and alleged misconduct."

Cross stood.

"Your Honor," he said, "before argument, the government requests the court take notice of supplemental filings submitted this morning."

The defense attorney rose immediately.

"Objection," he said. "We have not had time to review—"

"You will," Cross said calmly. "And you will understand why they could not wait."

The judge raised a hand.

"Mr. Cross," the judge said, "you are asking a great deal of patience from this court."

Cross nodded.

"And offering clarity in return," he said.

The judge hesitated, then nodded.

"Proceed," the judge said.

Cross opened his binder.

"Over the last seven years," Cross said, "a coordinated structure diverted federal funds through domestic programs and international partners under the guise of compliance."

The defense attorney scoffed.

"This is conjecture," he said.

Cross did not look at him.

"It is documentation," Cross said.

He placed a single exhibit on the table and slid it forward to the clerk.

The clerk glanced at it, then looked up sharply.

The judge leaned in.

"What am I looking at?" the judge asked.

"A directive," Cross said. "Issued outside formal channels. Referenced in internal correspondence across multiple agencies."

The defense attorney stepped forward.

"This document has no signature," he said. "No authority."

Cross turned at last.

"Authority," Cross said, "is demonstrated by obedience."

The room went still.

The judge studied the page.

"Counsel," the judge said to the defense, "have you seen this before?"

The defense attorney hesitated.

"No," he said.

Cross spoke again.

"Of course you have not," he said. "Because it was never meant for daylight."

He flipped another page.

"Here is the same language repeated in a transportation contract three states away," Cross said. "And here it is again in a healthcare funding memo."

He paused.

"Patterns are not coincidence," Cross said. "They are design."

The judge removed his glasses.

"You are alleging centralized coordination," the judge said.

"Yes," Cross replied.

"And judicial interference," the judge added.

"Yes," Cross said again.

A murmur rippled through the room.

The defense attorney leaned toward his client and whispered urgently.

The judge raised his gavel but did not strike it.

"I will not rule today," the judge said slowly. "But I will say this."

Everyone leaned forward.

"If even a fraction of what is alleged here is true," the judge said, "then this court has been misused."

Silence followed.

The judge looked directly at Cross.

"You understand the burden you have taken on," the judge said.

"I do," Cross replied.

"Then I advise you to meet it," the judge said.

He banged the gavel once.

"Court is adjourned."

The room erupted in movement.

Warren met Cross in the aisle.

"That went better than expected," she said.

"It went exactly as needed," Cross replied.

Outside the courtroom, a man slipped away down a side hall, phone already pressed to his ear.

"They showed the document," he said quietly.

Across town, a secure line lit up.

"So it is real," a voice said.

Another answered.

"Yes," came the reply. "And it is bigger than we thought."

Daniel Cross walked out into the afternoon light.

The hearing was over.

The reckoning was not.

End of Chapter Thirteen

Chapter Fourteen

The Collapse

It began quietly.

That was how collapses always began. Not with sirens or arrests, but with decisions made in private rooms by people who finally understood they were out of options.

At 6:42 a.m., a resignation letter hit an inbox in the capital.

At 6:58, a second followed.

By 7:15, a senior official closed his office door and did not reopen it.

Daniel Cross watched the updates scroll across his screen without reaction. He had learned to recognize the rhythm. When the center gave way, the edges followed.

Warren stood beside his desk, arms folded.

"Transportation director just stepped down," she said. "Medical oversight board dissolved its executive committee."

Cross nodded.

"They are trying to look decisive," he said.

"They are trying to look innocent," Warren replied.

Cross opened a new message.

CROSS: Prepare indictments three and four. Hold them.

Warren raised an eyebrow.

"You are not filing?" she asked.

"Not yet," Cross said. "Let them keep guessing."

Outside, reporters gathered. Questions sharpened. Statements grew shorter. No one smiled anymore.

In a quiet office two floors above the hearing room, the judge sat with his attorney, hands clasped so tightly they had gone white.

"They are abandoning you," the attorney said.

The judge stared at the wall.

"They said this would never surface," he murmured.

"They said many things," the attorney replied. "We need to prepare."

"For what?" the judge asked.

The attorney hesitated.

"For cooperation," he said.

The judge laughed once. Short. Hollow.

"Cooperate with who?" he asked.

"The truth," the attorney said.

The judge closed his eyes.

Across town, the woman who had delivered the documents watched the news alone in her apartment. She had not slept. She had not answered her phone.

Her name had not appeared.

Not yet.

She opened an email from Cross.

CROSS: You did the right thing.

She stared at the words for a long time.

Then she replied.

WOMAN: I know.

Back at the federal building, Cross's phone rang again.

This time, it was not a threat.

"This is counsel for Judge ," the voice said. "He wishes to discuss terms."

Cross closed his eyes briefly.

"Have him surrender his devices," Cross said. "Then we can talk."

Silence.

"I will relay that," the voice said.

The call ended.

Warren exhaled.

"That is it," she said.

"That is one of them," Cross replied.

The headlines grew bolder as the day wore on.

MULTIPLE OFFICIALS STEP DOWN AMID FEDERAL PROBE
SOURCES CONFIRM COOPERATION TALKS UNDERWAY

By evening, the system no longer pretended nothing was wrong.

Cross stood at the window as night fell, city lights flickering on like a map of nerves.

"They are collapsing inward," Warren said quietly.

"Yes," Cross replied. "Because outward would expose them."

He turned back to his desk and opened the final folder.

Title: Indictment Five.

He did not rush.

Some names deserved care.

Outside, somewhere deep inside a building that had never expected scrutiny, a shredder jammed.

It was too late.

The collapse had already started.

And there was only one chapter left.

End of Chapter Fourteen

Chapter Fifteen

The Verdict

The final filing went through at 9:02 a.m.

Daniel Cross watched the confirmation appear on his screen, then disappear beneath a stack of incoming alerts. He closed the laptop anyway. The work was done. What followed now belonged to the system he had challenged to remember what it was built for.

Outside, the city moved like any other morning. Coffee lines. Traffic reports. A normal day resting on an abnormal truth.

Warren entered quietly.

"It is official," she said. "Five indictments. Seventeen defendants. Three states cooperating. Two more negotiating."

Cross nodded.

"And the judge?" he asked.

"He surrendered everything," Warren replied. "Devices. Notes. Calendars. He wants immunity."

Cross considered that.

"He will not get it," he said.

"No," Warren agreed. "But he will talk."

Cross stood and buttoned his coat.

"Then the record will be complete," he said.

Across town, a press conference ended early. Questions went unanswered. Statements were read from paper and never lifted to eye level.

In another building, a senior official packed a box and left through a side door.

In a quiet apartment, the woman who had brought the documents turned off the television and sat in silence. For the first time in years, the weight on her chest felt lighter.

At noon, the headline settled in everywhere at once.

FEDERAL INDICTMENT UNRAVELS MULTI STATE FRAUD NETWORK SENIOR OFFICIALS AND JUDGE AMONG THOSE CHARGED

Daniel Cross read it once.

Then he closed the browser.

Warren watched him.

"You did it," she said.

Cross shook his head.

"No," he said. "The law did."

She smiled.

"You gave it a spine," she said.

Cross looked out the window.

"For a while," he said.

His phone buzzed one last time.

UNKNOWN NUMBER: This could have gone differently.

Cross typed a reply and sent it without hesitation.

CROSS: It went correctly.

He turned the phone face down.

Somewhere in a courthouse, a clerk filed documents that would be cited for decades. Somewhere else, a student would read about the case and believe, just a little, that the system could still work.

Cross picked up the blank folder from his desk. The one he had opened weeks ago with nothing inside.

He placed it in the drawer and closed it.

Outside, the city kept moving.

Inside the law, something had been restored.

Not perfection.
Accountability.

And that was enough.

End of Chapter Fifteen

                    THE END . . .For Now . . . .

Also by Roger Brantley

Gripping Southern Legal Thrillers That Break the Rules And the Internet

The Southern Order
The legal conspiracy that started it all. Dark secrets, deeper justice.

The Southern Defense
One defense attorney. One explosive case. One shot at redemption.

The Senator's Secret
Power. Corruption. And a marriage built on lies until now.

Bayou Verdict
A courtroom war in the heart of Louisiana. Everyone's watching the final verdict.

The Magnolia Trial
Old South power. New South revenge. One trial to rewrite history.

Case Dismissed in Baton Rouge
A small-town lawyer uncovers a billion-dollar cover-up. Justice was never part of the plan.

Orders from Barksdale
Military justice meets courtroom fire in this high-octane legal showdown.

Cold Case, Hot Verdict
A buried murder resurfaces in court and nothing is colder than the truth.

Madam Governor's Secret
She's one election away from power if her past doesn't destroy her first.

The Midland Trials
Two innocent men. One oilfield town. And a trial that shocks Texas.

Houston's Hung Jury
Twelve jurors. One billionaire defendant. And a verdict no one saw coming.

The Austin Appeal
When a case is too dangerous to close, the appeal is just the beginning.

Waco's Wrongful Suit
A broken system. A scandal worth millions. A lawsuit that could bring it all down.

Roger Brantley writes the most addictive legal thrillers in the South fast-paced, full of fire, and impossible to put down.

Made in the USA
Coppell, TX
18 January 2026

68586688R00075